Blackberries in the Dark

by Mavis Jukes
pictures by Thomas B. Allen

A YOUNG YEARLING BOOK

Published by
Dell Publishing Co., Inc.
1 Dag Hammarskjold Plaza
New York, New York 10017

Yearling ® TM 913705, Dell Publishing Co., Inc.

ISBN: 0-440-40647-1

Reprinted by arrangement with Alfred A. Knopf, Inc.

Printed in the United States of America

September 1987

10 9 8 7 6 5 4 3 2 1

W

For River, Amy, Cannon, Case, and Bob

—M.J.

For Jim Branch, Joe Kern, and B. Paty,
who taught me the art of fishing and so much more

—T.A.

When Austin got off the airplane, his grandmother was waiting for him—wearing a white linen suit and white linen shoes and a hat with artificial cherries on it.

"Hello, Austin," she said. They hugged. She smelled of flowers. "You've grown taller! How was the flight?"

"Fine," said Austin.

"You must be hungry."

"Not really," said Austin. "I ate on the plane." He swung his pack up onto one shoulder. They walked to the baggage claim, holding hands.

"My neighbor Wayne McCabe drove me to the airport to pick you up," said Austin's grandmother. "You remember Wayne. He's parked out front."

"Yup," said Austin.

"Wayne knows I don't like to drive myself places. He's been wonderful to me since Grandpa died."

Austin said nothing. His suitcase slid from the conveyor onto the carousel. He lifted it off when it came around.

"Out those doors," said Austin's grandmother, pointing. "You lead the way."

They stood on the sidewalk. "There's Wayne!" She waved at a black pickup. A tall man got out of the truck, wearing jeans and lizard-skin boots.

"Wayne, you remember Austin . . ."

"You've grown, boy," said Wayne to Austin. "How old are you now?"

"Nine," said Austin.

Wayne whistled. He tossed Austin's suitcase into the back of the truck.

Wayne helped Austin's grandmother into the cab. Austin climbed in beside her. His grandmother smiled at him and patted his knee. "So! We're on our own this summer. We've got ten days together. What shall we do?"

Austin stared at his hands in his lap.

"Want to come fly-fishing with me and the boys Saturday?" said Wayne. "We're going up to Two Rock."

Austin shrugged.

"Well, we'll see," said Austin's grandmother for Austin.

Wayne turned on the radio.

They headed out of town on a road that followed the river. After a few miles the pavement changed from asphalt to gravel.

"We're almost home," said Austin's grandmother as they clattered over a bridge.

Below them, Austin could see a man wearing green rubber waders standing in the river, fishing.

"Here we are," said Wayne as he pulled into the driveway. Austin stared through the windshield at the ranch. The grass around the barn was knee-deep and needed mowing.

"Thanks, Wayne," said Austin's grandmother.

"My pleasure," said Wayne. He got out and went around to help Austin's grandmother out of the cab. "Well, think about Saturday," he said to Austin. He leaned into the truck for Austin's bag.

"I don't think I'll go, but thanks anyway," said Austin. "And thanks for picking me up."

"Anytime," said Wayne.

He tipped his hat and got into his truck and backed out of the driveway.

"How come you didn't want to fish with Wayne and his boys?" said Austin's grandmother.

"I've never fished with anybody but Grandpa," Austin said. "Besides, it's fly-fishing. I don't know how to fly-fish."

"Neither do I," said Austin's grandmother. "Can't Wayne teach you?"

"I don't want Wayne to teach me," said Austin quietly. "Anyway, I guess I'll stick this stuff inside."

Austin carried his suitcase up the porch steps and through the kitchen and the living room into the spare bedroom. He put his suitcase and pack on the bed. The covers were folded down—the sheets were printed with cowboys. There were pictures of pheasants on the bedspread and on the curtains. He walked to the window and opened the curtains and looked outside.

He saw the swing that his grandfather had cut from a tire and hung from the maple tree.

"Do you want some lemonade?" his grandmother called from the kitchen.

Austin turned from the window. "Yes, please," he called back. He walked into the living room.

He opened the coat closet. It was empty of overcoats, empty of galoshes and wing-tip shoes. The old leather bag of golf clubs was gone.

He shut the door. He went over to the table and walked his fingers across the tablecloth and ate a handful of nuts out of the cut-glass bowl. He heard his grandmother stirring lemonade in the kitchen.

Austin peered into the corner cupboard. Through the glass door he could see his grandfather's fishing knife sitting on the edge of the shelf. Austin wondered why it was in the cupboard, by the teacups—instead of in his grandfather's fishing vest.

He opened the door. He took the pocketknife from the shelf and held it in his hand. He closed his fingers around the knife and then opened them up again. The handle of the knife was carved of antler, in the shape of a trout. Its sides were inlaid with turquoise spots with red centers—its eye was a fleck of gold. Austin put his thumbnail into the slot on the blade and slowly pulled it open. The blade was sharp. TESTED XX RAZOR EDGE was written in the steel. He looked at his reflection in the blade of the fishing knife. Then carefully, as his grandfather had taught him, he clicked it closed against his hand.

Austin put the knife back on the shelf and shut the cupboard door. He wandered over and played a few notes on the piano. "You didn't give away Grandpa's fishing stuff, did you?" he called.

"No," said his grandmother. She walked into the room carrying two aluminum glasses. "I haven't had the heart to go through the barn. Everything's in there, just like it was. Lemonade?"

They sat at the table drinking the lemonade and rattling the ice.

"But I've been through everything in the house, and that's been a job. And look what I found in the attic. . . ."

Austin's grandmother went over and opened the corner cupboard.

"I forgot I had it."

She stood on her tiptoes and carefully lifted something white down from behind the teacups. Austin moved closer to see what it was.

"It's an antique doll," she said, turning with the doll in her arms. "I played with it when I was a little girl." She tugged on the brim of the bonnet. She carefully arranged the doll's hair so that it fell behind its shoulders, and lowered the doll so Austin could see its face.

"It's a hundred years old," said his grandmother softly. "It's been passed from mother to daughter in my family for generations."

Austin stared at the doll's face. Its lips were pink and parted, and between them were white porcelain teeth. He gently made the eyes blink by moving one eyelid down with his finger.

"All the clothes are handmade," said Austin's grandmother. "See how delicately the lace was done in the old days?"

She lifted the doll's skirt to show the petticoat to Austin. Austin touched the slip. His fingernail looked dirty against the white.

"I didn't have a little girl to give it to—I had your father. And he had you. Now here the doll sits! Well, she's too old to be played with, anyway. Look at these," she whispered. "Do you know what these are?" She hooked her finger through the doll's necklace and pulled it up so Austin could see. "These are real coral beads. Aren't they lovely?"

Austin put his finger near his grandmother's finger and

pulled them a little closer. The thread on the necklace broke and the coral beads slid off the ends of the string and bounced and rolled on the floor.

"Here! I'll get a saucer!" said Austin's grandmother. She handed him the doll.

He put it on the couch.

She took a saucer from under a flowered teacup in the cupboard. They picked up the beads and put them on the saucer. "Now, there's a project," she told him. "There's a needle and white button thread in my sewing basket. You can

restring them while I change out of these clothes."

"Restring the beads?" said Austin. He looked over at the sewing basket. "How do I restring the beads?"

"String them on a needle and thread."

"I'm not good at threading needles, Gram—and I want to check the tractor. You still have it, don't you?"

"Of course I do," said Austin's grandmother. "It's been a while since it's been cranked up, but it's in the barn, right where Grandpa left it." She opened the corner cupboard and put the doll and the saucer of beads up onto the shelf.

Austin went outside.

He walked into the barn. The room was dim; it smelled of motor oil. It took his eyes a moment to get accustomed to the light.

Austin stood by his grandfather's workbench. Jars of nuts and screws were lined up along the back edge. Tools were hanging on the wall on nails. On the workbench was a wooden box filled with odds and ends, including a broken spinning reel.

There was a line of photographs stapled to the wall, all dusty and with curled edges—and all of Austin. He examined the most recent one. He was wearing black high-topped sneakers and his grandfather's New York Yankees cap, with the brim folded back. He was holding a German brown trout, his thumb looped through the gills.

Austin looked over at the Farmall Cub tractor. Behind it, where sunlight was leaking through the boards, Austin saw his grandfather's fishing gear: creel, rod, and rubber boots. His fishing vest and baseball cap were hanging from a nail.

"What are you thinking?" said Austin's grandmother from the doorway.

Austin stood with his back to his grandmother. "Nothing," he said, without turning to face her.

"Not thinking anything?"

"Well, I was thinking," he said after a moment, "about last summer." He paused. "About when Grandpa took me fishing. We stayed out late. We picked blackberries in the dark. We brought them home and you made that pie—and we ate it, in the middle of the night."

He looked down at the floor.

"He said this summer he'd teach me how to fly-fish at Two Rock Creek."

Austin's grandmother stood behind Austin. She put her hand on his shoulder.

Austin reached up and blotted his eyes with his sleeve. He turned to his grandmother. "And I was thinking," he said quietly, "about the day I wore Grandpa's baseball cap. He let me use his fishing knife—he showed me how to clean a trout."

"I remember that day," said Austin's grandmother. She bit her lip to keep her mouth from trembling.

"I didn't know—" began Austin.

His grandmother drew him near to her. "Nobody knew, Austin." She closed her eyes and shook her head. "Nobody knew that would be the last summer we'd all have together." She pressed Austin's cheek against her sweater and they stood there for a few minutes, rocking back and forth. After a while she asked:

"The day you wore the Yankees cap—was that the day you

and Grandpa thought that bull got through the fence? Remember you thought you heard the bull snort down by the creek—just after Grandpa caught that big German brown?"

Austin nodded into the front of her sweater.

"And it turned out to be something worse?"

Austin nodded again.

"What was it?"

"It was the game warden blowing his nose," said Austin. He looked up at his grandmother.

They both smiled a little. "Well, that was quite a day, wasn't it," said Austin's grandmother. "Here." She took off her apron and blew her nose in it and doubled it over and handed it to Austin. He blew his nose in the apron and wadded it up and handed it back.

"Well, we can still have blackberry pie," said Austin's grandmother. "How does that sound for dessert? Feel like picking?"

Austin nodded.

"You pick and I'll bake." She looked at her watch. "It's ten after six. But there's time, if you start out now. There's the can." She pointed out the doorway at a coffee can that was upside down on the fence post. Beside it a bird was warbling.

They walked outside. Austin took the can from the post. "You coming?" he asked.

Austin's grandmother looked down at her feet. "These shoes hurt my bunions. And anyway, I've got chicken to fry and corn to husk. And the laundry has to come in!" There was a row of cotton dresses clothespinned to the line. "You can make it, Austin. Just don't cross any fences."

There was a bull standing in the neighbor's field. It looked over at Austin, then lowered its enormous head to graze.

Austin waved to his grandmother. He drop-kicked the can and ran ahead to catch it. He started across the field. Above him the sky was an empty bowl of blue.

He stopped and looked back at the ranch. He saw his grand-mother standing by the barn door.

A grasshopper clicked onto his jeans, then popped away. He turned and looked for the bull.

It was gone.

Austin walked upward through the trees. At the top of the hill he stopped and listened. Below him he heard the rush of water. "Two Rock Creek," thought Austin.

He tramped through the woods until he came to the edge of a rocky stream bank and looked down at the water below.

There were blackberry bushes growing beside a boulder that rested in the creekbed.

Austin scrambled down the slope, making his way through the thick underbrush to the stream. He sat on the ground, tossing pebbles into the water. Then he stood up and began to fill the can with blackberries.

Suddenly, from the direction he had come, Austin heard the sounds of sticks cracking—as if something large was moving through the trees.

His heart raced. He climbed to the top of the boulder for a better look. He listened.

It was quiet. Mosquitoes drifted in the damp air.

After a while, Austin came down from the rock. He ate a few blackberries and then dropped a few into the can. Again he heard crashing on the ridge above. He whirled around and looked up.

The bushes were shaking.

A rock rolled down the bank.

For a long time Austin didn't move.

He heard the steady thud of approaching footsteps.

He crouched low and looked between the willow branches.

He heard himself breathing, so he held his breath to listen. Something else was breathing. Something was taking deep gasps of breath. He heard a grunt.

"Gram!" cried Austin. His grandmother stepped from the brush. "You made it!"

"I slipped up there and fell into some prickly bushes. Then these darn boots got mired in the mud."

Austin stared at his grandmother.

She was holding his grandfather's fishing rod and wearing his grandfather's green rubber boots and fishing vest. The creel was slung over her shoulder and across her chest.

And she was wearing the New York Yankees cap.

She took the cap from her head and put it on Austin's head. "There," she said, pulling the bill down over his nose. "You're set. Now, get to business." She leaned the rod against the boulder and put the creel on the ground. She took off the fishing vest and handed it to Austin.

Then, hoisting her hem above her knees, she waded out into the stream. "My, what a spot!" she called to Austin. "I haven't been here in years! I'd forgotten how beautiful it is!"

"Yup," said Austin. He laid the fishing vest down on the sand and searched the front pockets. He found a jar of Pautzke's salmon eggs, and he set it up on the boulder.

"There's no spool on the pole," called Austin's grandmother.

"You mean no spinning reel?" said Austin. He glanced over at the fishing rod. Then he snapped and unsnapped the vest pockets.

"It must be there," said Austin's grandmother.

"Here's some Wrigley's spearmint gum," said Austin. "And this." He held up an empty package of cigarettes, with two matches tucked behind the cellophane. Then he found a plastic flashlight and turned it on and off. "But no spinning reel," said Austin, looking in the back flap. "Rats."

He flipped open the lid of the fishing creel. Inside was a leather pouch.

"But there's a fly reel here, Gram." He frowned at the reel. "The problem is, how do we use it?"

Austin's grandmother waded to shore. Austin handed her the reel. "Let's see." She pulled on the leader and the reel clicked out leader and green line.

"I would say the spool goes here." She pointed to the cork handle on the rod.

Austin agreed.

They slid two copper rings around the reel at the base of the rod and fed the line up through the loops to the tip.

"Now we need the eggs," said Austin.

His grandmother picked up the jar. She unscrewed the cap and wrinkled her nose. She rolled two sticky eggs over the rim of the jar and into the lid and handed the lid to Austin.

She set the jar back on the rock, but it tipped and clattered down the side of the boulder. The eggs spilled out onto the sand like a broken strand of beads. They got down on their hands and knees to pick them up.

"There," said Austin's grandmother when the eggs were back in the jar. "Now how do we put them on the line? Aren't we supposed to have a float?"

"We tie on an egg hook and bite on some sinkers," Austin told her. He stood up and took two pine needles out of her hair. He patted her back. Then he searched the fishing vest again.

"Bad news," Austin reported after peering into a tiny empty plastic box. "We're out of egg hooks. But look!" He opened a silver tin and showed it to his grandmother. "Flies!"

They stared at the colored fishing flies.

"Flies that Grandpa tied," said Austin. "Do you think we could fly-fish?"

"I don't see why not," said Austin's grandmother.

They sat down beside each other on the damp ground, examining the fly box. There were rows of black hooks with wings of fuzz and feathers, all wrapped with shiny thread. "Look how little they are. Look how he wound the thread," said Austin.

"I always said Grandpa would have made a good seamstress," said Austin's grandmother. She took the tin box and selected a fly with an iridescent body and black wings. "Let's try this one." She dropped it lightly into Austin's hand.

"Thread it through, like threading a needle," she suggested to Austin. "Then we'll figure out a knot."

"I'm not good at threading needles," said Austin.

"I'll supervise," she told him. "Give it a whirl."

Austin folded back the brim of the baseball cap. He moved his tongue to the corner of his mouth and bit it softly. He shut one eye. He held the leader and the fly close to the end of his nose.

"Don't bite your tongue off," said Austin's grandmother.

Austin smiled.

He kept concentrating on the eye of the hook. "Did it!" he whispered a moment later. "Now, you tie the knot!"

Austin's grandmother carefully took the fly from Austin and pinched it between two fingers and then tipped her head back so she could see through the bottom of her glasses. She fed the leader farther through the eye of the hook and twirled it a few times and wound it around and through.

"A crochet knot," she announced after she had tightened it. "Modified. But no telling how it will hold in plastic. Give it a go!"

Holding the fly in one hand and the rod in the other, Austin walked to the edge of the water. He let the fly drift downstream, letting out line. Then he reeled it in. "I don't think this is how you do it," he said. He let it float down, again and again.

"It's beginning to get dark," said Austin's grandmother. "And I've chicken to fry—and a pie to bake!"

Austin looked over at his grandmother. "Let's stay and fish," he said. "The flashlight works. And we can just eat blackberries for supper."

"Good idea," said his grandmother. "Blackberries in the dark! It's a family tradition." She popped two blackberries into her mouth. "Heck with the pie," she told him. "We'll bake together another time." She ate blackberries, one after another, while Austin stood in the stream fishing.

She waded into the stream with a handful of berries for Austin.

"Thanks," said Austin. "Your turn." He traded the rod for the blackberries. "But wait! The fly is caught." He waded downstream and pulled the line free of some willows.

His grandmother began to reel it in, with a leaf attached.

As she was reeling, the leaf disappeared under the water. "This is harder than it looks," she told Austin. He was reaching for a cluster of berries.

The line grew tight.

"It's caught on the bottom," she said.

He turned around.

"It's caught on something." She stepped forward into the stream. The line got suddenly loose. "Never mind," she told Austin.

The tip of the fishing rod began to bend as she reeled again. "Well, hell's bells!" said Austin's grandmother. "I think we've got a fish!"

A trout was thrashing in the water a few feet ahead of her.

"Keep the tip up!" cried Austin. "Keep reeling and keep the tip up!"

"Help!" said Austin's grandmother. "Where's the net?"

"No net!" cried Austin. "Just pull the fish out of the water!"

"Pull it out? *You* pull it out!"

They both lifted the rod. The fish splashed out of the water, arching wildly in the air, on the end of the line.

They swung it onto the bank.

It flipped over and over in the sand and in the moss, slapping its body against the ground. Finally Austin grabbed it. "Get the hook out of its jaw!"

Austin watched it gulp air with its pink gills while his grandmother worked to unset the hook. "It's a brook trout," she told him. "What a beauty! See the blue spots? See the

red centers?" She pushed the barb backward through the trout's bottom lip. "Ouch!" she said, for the fish. "Now what?"

"Let's throw it back," said Austin. "Okay? It's good luck to throw back the first fish of the season. Grandpa said."

"Good idea," said Austin's grandmother. "Let's let it go."

Austin knelt down at the edge of Two Rock Creek. With both of his hands in the water, he gently released the trout into the stream. It darted away into the shadows.

He stood up and dried his hands on the back of his jeans. He looked at his grandmother. "Grandpa would like us doing this—wouldn't he," said Austin. "He would be happy we're learning to fly-fish at Two Rock Creek."

"Yes," said Austin's grandmother. "And tomorrow we'll learn how to drive the tractor." Austin's eyes grew wider. "You think we can't start that tractor?"

"I think we can start the tractor," said Austin. "And I think we can mow the grass around the barn."

"*And* we can fly-fish, so Saturday we're going with Wayne," said Austin's grandmother. She put everything back into the fishing-vest pockets and handed the vest to Austin. "Here. You put this on."

She helped Austin into the vest. Then she picked up the creel and the fishing rod.

Austin followed his grandmother up the stream bank. "I skidded down this on the way over," she huffed. "Rump over teakettle!" She offered her hand to Austin and they helped each other over the top. They threaded their way through the woods between black oaks and pines.

Austin walked beside his grandmother as they crossed the fields to the ranch. Her boots squeaked and thumped.

When they reached the house, Austin's grandmother flopped into the wicker chair on the porch. "I set something in the corner cupboard for you, Austin," she said. "It belonged to someone special for many years. It's really not something for a boy to have—but still and all, I want it to be yours. Go and find it!"

"Okay," said Austin.

"But promise me you'll handle it carefully—it's not something to play with."

"I promise," said Austin.

He went into the house and turned on the kitchen light. He took off the fishing vest and the Yankees cap and hung them on the doorknob. He turned on the living room light and opened the corner cupboard. He saw teacups and saucers. He saw his grandfather's fishing knife sitting on the edge of the shelf.

"Can you reach it?" called his grandmother from the porch.

"Yup," said Austin.

For a long while the house was quiet. Austin's grandmother sat on the porch in the dark. Then she opened the screen door and clumped into the kitchen. She took off the rubber boots and stood them up on the linoleum near the fishing vest and the baseball cap. She set the creel on the counter.

Then, in her stocking feet, Austin's grandmother walked

through the kitchen into the living room. She glanced over at the corner cupboard. The fishing knife was still on the shelf.

"Austin?"

"In here," said Austin.

He was sitting on the edge of the bed. Beside him was the saucer of beads. He had threaded a needle and was knotting the thread. Leaning against the cowboy pillow case was the antique doll. The brim of her bonnet was turned back. She was watching Austin, with blue glass eyes.

"She's supervising," said Austin.

His grandmother stood there, with her hands in her sweater pockets, staring at the antique doll. "So I see."

Austin looked up. "Thank you," he told her.

His grandmother smiled. "Well! I'm glad you found each other."

She sat next to Austin on the bed and carefully took the needle from him. She set it on the saucer, among the coral beads.

"And Austin—"

She picked up Austin's hand and pressed the pocketknife into his palm, and closed his fingers around it.

"This is yours, too."

47